Vincent, Theo and the Fox

A mischievous adventure through the paintings of
Vincent van Gogh

By Ted Macaluso

Illustrations by Vincent van Gogh

Owls Cove Press
Reston, Virginia

To Mark and Alexandra, with love.

Originally published 2014, updated December 2018

Text Copyright ©2014, 2018 by Theodore F. Macaluso

Published by Owls Cove Press
Reston, Virginia
OwlsCovePress@gmail.com.

Font: Kohinoor Devanagari

When he was a boy, Vincent van Gogh liked to go for walks with his young brother, Theo. Pausing to watch farmers harvest their crops, the two boys talked about what they wanted to be when they grew up.

"I'm going to be a teacher when I grow up," said Vincent, "or maybe a minister, like Father."

"If you want," said Theo, "but do you know when I see you look your happiest? It's when you are drawing on your sketchpad."

Before Vincent could reply, the two boys saw a fox sneak into the blue cart below them. The fox found a farmer's lunch bag and started to rip it open.

"That fox should be careful – the farmer will shoot him," said Vincent.

"Let's catch him," replied Theo, "and take him someplace safe."

So Vincent and Theo crawled under the picket fence and through the green brambly bushes. When they got near the blue cart, the brothers tried to pounce. But the fox jumped out of the cart and ran down the road as fast as he could go.

Vincent and Theo ran after him.

The fox ran to a village. He saw a yellow house next to a restaurant. Boy, was he hungry.

The fox was young. That morning, he had left home determined to learn his way in the world. "I shall be like a human and eat in that restaurant," he thought. The fox went inside.

The restaurant was empty. A waiter was setting tables, his back to the fox. The fox had never been in a restaurant. He said to himself, "Humans must eat the colorful flowers on the tables."

The fox jumped on a table and dishes fell to the floor. The waiter turned and gave a loud shout. Vincent and Theo appeared at the door. "There he is," yelled Vincent, "get him!"

Quick as a fox can be, the creature ran between the waiter's legs, through the kitchen and out the back door. "A fox should not eat in a restaurant," he thought.

Vincent and Theo ran through the kitchen and tumbled out the back door after the fox. They chased the fox across a sandy, windswept field. After a while, they came to the ocean. The fox was on the beach.

"We can trap him," yelled Theo. Vincent ran to the left side of the beach; Theo ran to the right. The boys started closing in on the fox from each side. But the quick-witted animal jumped into the water and swam to the boat. Before anyone could stop him, the fox gnawed through the anchor rope. The boat drifted away. The boys ran down the beach, following the boat and the fox.

At first, the fox loved the rocking of his boat and the snap of wind in the sails. "I am a sailor," he thought proudly. However, the sky grew dark. The fox could not control the rudder. Water drenched the boat. "A fox should not be at sea," he thought, "a fox belongs on the land."

When the boat drifted to shore the fox jumped out and started running.

He ran until he saw some thatched cottages by a hill.

The fox crept towards the small cottage on the left. He was still hungry. He did not see Vincent and Theo, who were still trying to catch him.

The fox snuck into the cottage. In one room he saw a woman working by the fireplace.

In another, he saw paintbrushes in a pot and empty cups. The fox

thought, "Where is the food?"

Creeping quietly, the fox came to the back room. He saw people eating potatoes.

"They like this food," he thought, "I shall be a potato eater too."

On silent, padded paws the fox jumped to the kitchen counter, where there was a basket of potatoes. He took one and ate it.

"Pretty good, but not as good as a field mouse," he thought. He took another. "Pretty good, but not as good as a field mouse," he thought again. The fox reached for one more. "Pretty good, but not.... Yikes!" The basket tipped over. With a clang and a clatter, the potatoes spilled everywhere.

One of the women looked over and saw the fox. She nudged her husband. "I shall catch that fox," her husband said. "We shall eat him for supper. Later I will make you a fur coat." The man stood.

The fox saw Theo looking through the back door. "A fox does not belong in a house," he thought. The fox ran for his life, faster than fast. Vincent and Theo were close on his heels.

The fox ran until he came to a city. Vincent and Theo paused to catch their breath. "Look down below," said Vincent, "that fox is walking up the street!" The boys followed. They were growing tired by the time they reached the street.

"My feet hurt," cried Theo. "My shoes are worn out from chasing that fox."

They stopped in front of a cobbler shop and gazed longingly at a new pair of leather clogs.

Vincent thought of his bed back home and how nice it would be to lie in it.

Meanwhile, the fox was tired too. The noise and smells of the city scared him.

He saw woods on the far side of the city and ran toward them. He was almost there when he heard a shout behind him. Vincent and Theo had caught up. The fox plunged into the woods.

Vincent and Theo followed the fox, dodging between the trees. At the far edge of the woods, they saw the fox crawl into a sunny field and disappear.

The brothers stopped. "I think the fox has found a safe home," said Vincent. "Yes," replied Theo. "It's getting late. Why don't we go home now?"

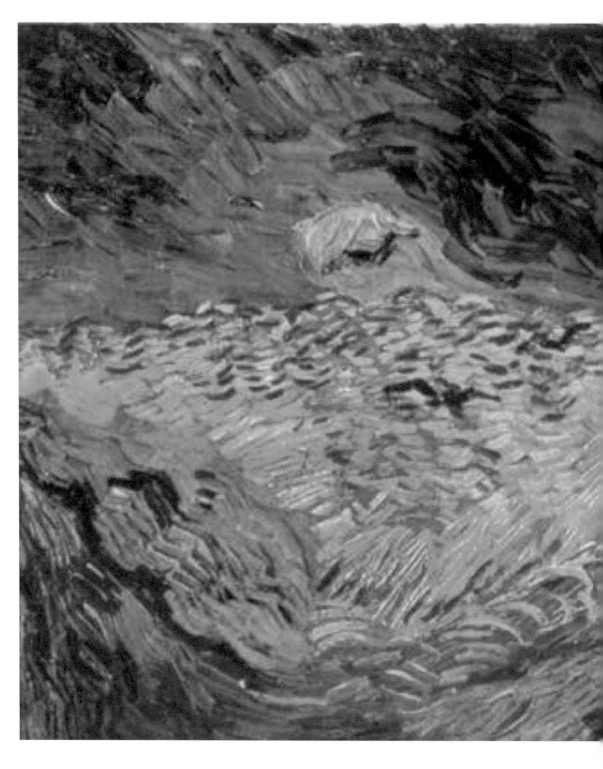

As the day drew to a close, the fox walked through a golden field.

Crows flew out of his way, slowly circling in the sky.

"I'm happy here. This is where a fox should be," he thought.

As the brothers walked home, Theo said, "That fox was young. He wanted to try everything. But he could not order food in a restaurant; he was a poor sailor, and a clumsy potato eater. Still, I believe he had to try those things before he could know what makes him happy."

Sometimes, you can't know if a choice is right, unless you try it," Vincent replied. As they walked, Vincent tried to imagine what he might look like as an adult. He thought of what he might want to be. There were so many choices.

He thought about being a pastor of a small church like his Father.

Vincent wondered whether he would grow up to mend roads...

...or plow fields.

He thought of being a lieutenant in a distant army, a postman close to home or a banker walking to work in a grey felt hat.

For a short time, Vincent even thought about running away to join a gypsy camp.

And he thought about what it would mean to be a painter. He thought about standing at an easel in a studio. Then he thought about carrying an easel and paint to capture the landscapes he and Theo had seen.

Finally, he said, "I may try different things when I grow up, just like the fox." He turned to Theo and said, "I will search until I find work that makes me happy."

"I'll help you, whatever you choose," said Theo.

That night, asleep in his bed, Vincent dreamt of the beautiful places he and Theo had seen that day. Vincent smiled. In his dream, he saw the fox was happy, running through fields and hills, wild and free under the starry sky.

Epilogue

Vincent Van Gogh grew up to be one of the world's greatest painters. He was born March 30, 1853 in Groot-Zundert, a small village in Holland. Theo was born four years later, on May 1, 1857.

Vincent started drawing at an early age. He drew this sketch - The Goat Herd - when he was only 10.

However, like the fox in the story, Vincent tried many different jobs before he became a painter. At the age of 16, with his Uncle's help, Vincent was apprenticed to an art dealer in The Hague. While this job let Vincent visit many museums and art galleries, in the end it didn't work out. When he was 23, Vincent resigned and took a new job as a teacher. Within a year, he left to work in a bookshop and, later, as a minister in a poor coal-mining district in Belgium. He was unhappy with all those jobs too.

In March 1880, when he was about to turn 27, Vincent's interest in art was renewed. From that point on, Vincent painted with all his heart. His goal was to paint so that the viewer would feel the emotions Vincent felt. To do this, he used heavy paint with bold strokes and colors. He did it so well that his paintings survive over time and speak to us today, over 140 years later.

Vincent lived only 10 more years, but in that time, he created over 2,000 paintings and drawings. He also wrote nearly 700 letters to his brother Theo, which tell us about his paintings and life. Theo helped him always, sending money to buy paint and help with rent and food.

Vincent's art was ahead of its time. During his life, he sold just a few paintings and bartered some others for food and necessities. Most of his paintings were sold after his death. Today his paintings sell for millions of dollars. Most of his paintings are in museums around the world and are too priceless to sell.

Author's note

The story was inspired when my son was five years old. He asked me to read him the monograph from an exhibit at the National Gallery of Art: *Van Gogh's Van Goghs: Masterpieces from the Van Gogh Museum Amsterdam* by Richard Kendall with contributions by John Leighton and Sjraar van Heugten (National Gallery of Art, Washington, D.C.; 1998; ISBN 0-89468-237-7). Many of the paintings in this story were included in the exhibit. The exhibit is on virtual tour at http://www.nga.gov/exhibitions/vginfo.htm.

If you are interested in studying van Gogh's art in more detail, there is a wealth of both information and images at www.vggallery.com. Both www.wikipaintings.org and www.awesome-art.com also have many images.

There is a lot more information out there. Look around – and don't forget the Van Gogh Museum where the originals of many of the paintings in the story can be found! http://www.vangoghmuseum.nl/vgm/index.jsp

Before You Leave

Thank you for taking this imaginary journey with me. You could have chosen from many picture books on art I appreciate your picking this one.

Authors live and die by reviews. Tell both me and potential future readers what you think. Just search Amazon.com and/or GoodReads.com for "Vincent Theo Fox" to leave your review. I would appreciate it a lot.

If you want to learn about other books I write, please check out my website at www.tedmacaluso.com.

- Ted Macaluso

List of Illustrations

The names of the paintings and drawings (with the city and year they were created) are listed below, in their order of appearance. Van Gogh's paintings are not always given the same title. For consistency, I have used the titles found on the web site http/www.awesome-art.com since most of the paintings and sketches in the story can be found there. Some of the art is from www.wikipaintings.org/en/vincent-van-gogh in which case I used their title (indicated by a "W" after the year of creation).

<u>Cover:</u>

Landscape from Saint Rémy/Mountainous Landscape Behind Saint-Paul Hospital (Saint-Rémy, June 1889)

<u>Text:</u>

Harvest at La Crau, with Montmajour in the Background (Arles, June 1888); Vincent's House in Arles – The Yellow house (Arles, September 1888); Interior of a Restaurant (Paris, June-July 1887); View of the Sea at Scheveningen (The Hague, August 1882); Seascape at Saintes-Maries (Saintes-Marie-de-la-mer, 1888 - W);

Fishing Boats on the Beach at Saintes-Maries (Saintes-Marie-de-la-mer, 1888); Thatched Cottages by a Hill (Saint- Rémy, 1890); Peasant Woman by the Fireplace (Netherlands, 1885); Still Life with Paintbrushes in a Pot (Nuenen, November 1884 - W); The Potato Eaters (Nuenen, April 1885); Basket of Potatoes (Nuenen, September 1885 - W); Head of a Peasant Woman with White Cap (Nuenen, 1885 – W); View of Roofs and Backs of Houses (Paris, Spring, 1886); A Pair of Shoes (experts disagree: some say Paris, 1886, others say Nuenen, 1885); A Pair of Leather Clogs (Arles, March 1888); Vincent's Bedroom (Arles, October 1888);

Trees and Undergrowth (Paris, Summer, 1887); Tree Trunks with Ivy (Saint-Rémy, July 1889); Sunny Lawn in a Public Park (Arles, Bouches-du-Rhône, 1888); Wheatfield (Auvers-sur-Oise, July 1890); Landscape with the Chateau of Auvers at Sunset (Auvers-sur-Oise, June 1890); The Church at Auvers (Auvers-sur-Oise, June 1890); The Road Menders (Saint-Rémy, November 1889); Field with Ploughman and Mill (Saint-Rémy, October 1889); Portrait of Milliet, Second Lieutenant of the Zouaves (Arles, September 1888); Portrait of the Postman Joseph Roulin (Arles, August 1888); Self Portrait with Grey Felt Hat (Paris, 1886/1887); Encampment of Gypsies with Caravans (Arles, August 1888); Self Portrait in Front of the Easel (Paris, 1888); Self Portrait on the Road to Tarascon – The Painter on his way to Work (Arles, July 1888 - W); Starry Night (Saint-Rémy, June 1889); The Goat Herd (Zundert, October 1862)

Made in United States
Troutdale, OR
10/11/2023

13593911R00024